GRANNY ANL

Penelope Farmer has written several fantasy stories for young people, such as *A Castle of Bone*, *Thicker Than Water* and *Charlotte Sometimes*, which inspired a popular song of the same name by The Cure. Her first published stories were written when she was fifteen and were followed a few years later by her first novel for children, *Summer Birds*, which was runner-up for the Carnegie Medal. For Walker, she has written *Twin Trouble*, and she is also the author of a number of books for adults. She has two grown-up daughters and grandchildren.

*Ellie ran out of the room and down
the stairs in time to meet Granny.*

Granny and Me

Written by
PENELOPE FARMER

Illustrated by
VALERIE LITTLEWOOD

WALKER BOOKS
AND SUBSIDIARIES

LONDON • BOSTON • SYDNEY

For Eleanor Ruth Penelope

First published 1998 by Walker Books Ltd
87 Vauxhall Walk, London SE11 5HJ

This edition published 1998

2 4 6 8 10 9 7 5 3

Text © 1998 Penelope Farmer
Illustrations © 1998 Valerie Littlewood

The right of Penelope Farmer to be identified as author
of this work has been asserted by her in accordance with the
Copyright, Designs and Patents Act 1988.

This book has been typeset in Plantin Light.

Printed in England by Clays Ltd, St Ives plc

British Library Cataloguing in Publication Data
A catalogue record for this book is
available from the British Library.

ISBN 0-7445-6043-8

CONTENTS

When the new baby wasn't crying he was feeding.
And when he wasn't feeding he was asleep.

GRANNY GOES CLIMBING

Ellie had been looking forward to the new baby, Adam.

"You're my big girl now, Ellie," Mum said.

"You'll be able to help Mum look after the baby, won't you, Ellie?" Dad said.

Ellie knew the baby would be little at first – too little to play with. But she hadn't realized just how little he would be, and just how long she'd have to wait before she could play with him.

"He's always crying," she said crossly. For so he was. And when he wasn't crying he was feeding. And when he wasn't feeding he was asleep. Or dirtying his nappy. Or being sick. Mum was so busy looking after Adam, she was often too tired to play with Ellie.

"Ssh, Ellie," she said, when Ellie sang – very loudly – a new rhyme she'd learned at playschool. "Sshh! You'll wake the baby."

"That's naughty, Ellie," Dad said, when Ellie got out her paints and painted a picture on the floor. "Mum's much too busy with the baby to clear up messes like that."

"The baby makes messes, too. Horrid messes. When's he going to go away?" asked Ellie.

She went up to her bedroom to find her favourite teddy. Granny had knitted him from bright blue wool. His name was Teddy Taylor.

"Let's see if Granny's coming, Teddy," she said. "Granny won't be too tired to play with us."

Ellie and Teddy Taylor looked out of the

window. But Granny wasn't coming along the street yet.

Dad had put bars on the window so Ellie couldn't fall out on to the little roof below. She was much too big to squeeze between the bars. Teddy Taylor wasn't too big, though. Feeling cross with the baby made her feel cross with him as well.

"I'm going to throw you out of the window, Teddy Taylor," she said.

And so she did. And there sat Teddy Taylor on the roof all by himself.

Doesn't he look lonely? Ellie thought. So she fetched her other teddy, Fenchurch Bear. She pushed him through the bars. And now Teddy Taylor and Fenchurch Bear were sitting on the roof together, side by side.

I like throwing bears out of the window, Ellie thought. But she didn't have any more bears.

She had Maribel Doll, though. So she threw Maribel Doll out too. What about Stripy Tiger? she thought. Out went Stripy Tiger. And out went Platypus. And out went Mr McTavish, the Scottie dog. And out went Sailor Boy. And out went Floppy Bunny and Nelly the Elephant. In the end all her animals and dolls were sitting on the roof, except for Russia Doll. Ellie threw her a bit too hard. Russia Doll rolled right the way down the roof and fell off.

Ellie was frightened when she saw Russia Doll fall down. Suppose Russia Doll broke, she thought. Then she heard Dad coming up the stairs. Would Dad be cross with her, she wondered? She sat on the floor and pretended to be playing with her Legoland train set. Perhaps he wouldn't notice the toys sitting on the roof.

But Dad was carrying Russia Doll.

"What's this, Ellie?" he asked. "Did you throw her out of the window?" And he went over to the window straight away to shut it. So he saw Teddy Taylor and Fenchurch Bear, Maribel Doll, Stripy Tiger, Platypus, Mr McTavish, Sailor Boy, Floppy Bunny and Nelly the Elephant lying on the roof.

"Oh, Ellie," he said. "Oh, Ellie, you naughty girl. What will Mum say?"

Then he said, "Well, Ellie, how are you going to get those toys back in again?"

Ellie hadn't thought of that. Because of the bars, of course, no one could get out of the window from her room to fetch them. And the roof was too high from the ground for Dad to be able to climb up.

"I don't know," she said in a small voice. And suddenly she didn't think it was fun any more. She wanted Teddy Taylor and Fenchurch Bear and Maribel Doll and Stripy

Tiger and Platypus and Mr McTavish and Sailor Boy and Floppy Bunny and Nelly the Elephant sitting on her bed as usual so she could cuddle them before she went to sleep.

Dad put Russia Doll back on the bed. She looked lonely. She made Ellie feel lonely too. Ellie stared and stared out of the window trying to think of some way to rescue all the toys. But she couldn't think of anything.

Dad said, "Well, Ellie. I think those toys will have to stay outside, don't you?"

"Suppose it rains?" said Ellie. "Suppose they all get wet?"

"You should have thought of that," said Dad.

Ellie could see a big cloud coming up. She was sure it was going to rain any minute. She didn't want Teddy Taylor and the others to get wet. She began to cry.

Dad picked her up and gave her a hug. But

he still said, "*I'm* not going to get them in."

Ellie stared out of the window again. Teddy Taylor was looking sad, she thought. And Fenchurch Bear was looking cross. Just then, though, Ellie saw someone coming up the street. Someone wearing an orange and purple striped coat and purple trousers. Only one person she knew wore clothes like that.

"Granny!" she shouted. "Granny's coming." And she ran out of the room and down the stairs in time to meet Granny coming in at the front door. Most of the visitors who came these days wanted to see baby Adam first. But Granny didn't. Instead of going into the sitting-room, where Mum and the new baby were, she went straight upstairs with Ellie to see all Ellie's animals and dolls sitting on the roof.

"Oh, you silly Ellie," she said, laughing.

"Haven't you been having fun!"

"But I don't want them outside any more," said Ellie, beginning to cry again.

"Of course you don't," said Granny. "And I know just the person to help. Look out of the window, Ellie, and in a moment I'll have a surprise for you."

Ellie watched Granny's striped coat and purple trousers disappearing down the street. And then she watched for them coming back. But she didn't see them coming back. Not at first. What she saw was a big ladder walking up the street. In a moment she saw a big man behind the ladder, carrying it. And in another moment she saw Granny's bright clothes following along behind.

Ellie ran downstairs. Mum came out of the sitting-room carrying the baby. Dad came too, and opened the front door just as

Granny and the man and the ladder arrived.

"This is Jim the window-cleaner," said Granny. "If you ask him very nicely, Ellie, I think his ladder might help us rescue Teddy Taylor and his friends."

"Oh please," said Ellie, looking at Granny and Jim.

Jim set the ladder against the wall. And Granny said, "I need some climbing practice. I'm off to climb a mountain on Saturday. Jim will hold the ladder for me, won't you, Jim?" The next moment she was running up the ladder while all the rest of them stood underneath and watched.

"Don't fall, Granny," said Ellie anxiously.

"Of course I'm not going to fall," said Granny, shinning expertly on to the roof. "Here, catch."

The next minute Teddy Taylor came sailing down, followed by Fenchurch Bear.

The next minute Teddy Taylor came sailing down,
followed by Fenchurch Bear.

Dad caught Teddy Taylor. Jim the window-cleaner caught Fenchurch Bear. Ellie missed catching Maribel Doll. But Mum picked her up and dusted her down so that was all right. And in a moment Stripy Tiger, Mr McTavish, Platypus, Sailor Boy, Floppy Bunny and Nelly the Elephant were safely on the ground again, too. And so was Granny.

"Can I climb the ladder?" asked Ellie.

"No," said Mum and Dad and Jim. And baby Adam began to cry.

"Ellie'd be quite safe if I held her feet," begged Granny.

"All right," said Mum.

So Ellie climbed five rungs of the ladder with Granny holding her feet, and felt quite safe. It was like going on the climbing-frame at playschool, but higher. "Now I'm taller than you, Dad!" she shouted. "And much,

much taller than baby Adam," she added, so softly that only Granny heard.

"Of course you are," whispered Granny.

Afterwards Ellie took Teddy Taylor and Fenchurch Bear and Maribel Doll and Stripy Tiger and Platypus and Mr McTavish and Sailor Boy and Floppy Bunny and Nelly the Elephant upstairs and put them back on their bed, alongside Russia Doll. They looked very happy and good as new. The big cloud had gone away. It hadn't rained on them after all.

"I promise I won't throw you out again," said Ellie. And then she whispered, "But we did climb the ladder, Granny and me. And one day, Granny says, we'll climb a real mountain together. Just Granny and me."

GRANNY GOES TO THE FETE

Almost every day Mum and Ellie and baby Adam went out for a walk in the park. Ellie used to go in the pushchair but she was too big now, so she walked. Sometimes she pushed Russia Doll in her pushchair. Adam rode in his sling on Mum's front. He was too little to see out and anyway he was asleep most of the time. Even when he was awake he didn't cry. Sometimes Ellie took Teddy Taylor in a sling on her front. He didn't cry either. So, for once, Mum and Ellie were able to have a good talk. Ellie liked going in the park with Mum and baby Adam.

Every day they passed the fence which

bordered the school garden. One day there was a big notice tied all the way along it. Ellie couldn't read the words. But she could see the pictures of balloons and clowns.

"The school is going to have a fête next Saturday," Mum said.

"What's a fête?" asked Ellie.

"Well," said Mum, "it's a sort of big outside party. People sell things like books and toys and cakes. And there are games to play, and sometimes a bouncy castle."

"And balloons and clowns?" asked Ellie.

"Sometimes they have balloons and clowns," said Mum.

"Can we go to the fête?" asked Ellie.

Granny came to tea that day. She was wearing shiny pink trainers and a shirt with an elephant on it.

"On Saturday, we're going to the fête,"

said Ellie. "There's going to be a bouncy castle and clowns and balloons."

"There might be clowns and balloons and a bouncy castle," warned Mum. "I'm only guessing."

"Of course there's going to be a bouncy castle," said Granny. "Can I come too, Ellie's mum?"

"Yes," nodded Mum, looking pleased.

On Saturday, Mum and Dad, Ellie, Adam in his sling on Dad's front and Teddy Taylor in his sling on Ellie's front set out for the fête in the school garden. Granny met them at the school gate.

It was a lovely day. Ellie and Adam were wearing their sunhats. Granny was wearing a sunhat too, but her sunhat looked big enough for two grannies. It was pink, like her shiny trainers. Granny liked the colour pink.

Ellie couldn't see a bouncy castle at first. But there *were* big bunches of balloons tied to the fence. And there *were* two clowns, a big one and a little one. The big one was riding a bike with one wheel. The little one was juggling with three balls. Or rather he was trying to juggle. He wasn't very good at it. Often he dropped the balls. When the children laughed at him, he threw the balls at them. He threw one ball at Ellie. It was a very soft ball. She threw it to Granny. Granny threw it back at the clown. And then she went over to the clown and said, "Let me try."

"All right," said the clown. His mouth was painted to look as if it was smiling. But his voice didn't sound smiley. It sounded cross. He pointed at Granny's sunhat.

"Won't that get in the way?" he asked.

"No problem," said Granny, taking off her

The little clown was juggling with three balls.
Or rather he was trying to juggle.

big pink sunhat. The next minute there she was in her pink trainers juggling with all three balls. She didn't drop any.

"Do you want me to teach you how to do it?" she asked the clown.

"No thanks," said the little clown. And the big clown on the one-wheeled bicycle rode away, fast.

"Perhaps he thinks you want to ride his bike, too," said Mum.

"No thanks," said Granny. "I only ride bicycles with two wheels."

Mum bought a jar of jam from one stall. She bought a plant with ferny leaves from another. Dad guessed the weight of a big cake with white icing on it. He threw hoop-la rings on to a stick – one, two, three, four – and won a pink vase as a prize.

He gave the vase to Granny. "It goes with your hat," he said.

Granny went away then. Mum began looking at a stall with books on it. Ellie was bored now. "Where's the bouncy castle?" she asked. Because she still couldn't see it.

"Perhaps there isn't one," sighed Mum.

Just then Granny came back. "I've found the bouncy castle," she said. "Come on, Ellie. Mum and Dad can look after Adam. But you can look after me." She took Ellie's hand, and off they went to find, sure enough, a big red, blue and yellow bouncy castle. There were lots of children there jumping up and down. So many that Granny said, "Perhaps I won't go on the bouncy castle. I might break my new pink vase. And I think I'm a bit too big."

"I think you are a bit too big, too," said Ellie. "But I'm not too big."

She and Teddy Taylor bounced on the bouncy castle for a long, long time. Granny didn't say, "Come on, Ellie, haven't you been on the bouncy castle long enough?" Or, "Come on, Ellie, it's time for tea." Or, "Come on, Ellie, it's time to go home." Ellie and Teddy Taylor got tired of bouncing on the bouncy castle long before Granny got tired of watching them.

"Are you sure you don't want to stay on the bouncy castle any longer?" Granny asked. "You can bounce a bit more if you like."

"No thanks," said Ellie firmly. "I want to do something else now."

"How about having your face painted?" said Granny, pointing at a long queue.

Ellie had seen some children on the bouncy castle with faces painted to look like dogs or dragons or ghosts or pirates. But she didn't know she could have her face painted too. "Yes please," she said.

It was a long queue, though. Granny

bought Ellie a green iced lolly so she wouldn't get bored while she was waiting. She bought a pink iced lolly for herself.

"It goes with your hat and shoes," said Ellie.

"I think I might like the *taste* of pink, too," said Granny.

"I like the taste of pink *and* green," Ellie said.

Ellie ate most of Granny's iced lolly as well as her own. By the time she had finished them she was at the head of the queue for face painting.

"What are you going to be, Ellie?" Granny asked. "A dog? A clown? A tabby cat?"

"I want to be a tiger," said Ellie. "A tiger with stripes."

So Ellie had stripes, whiskers and a tiger nose painted on her face. She looked just like a tiger, she thought, when the painting lady showed her her face in the mirror. "Can Teddy Taylor be a tiger too?" she asked Granny.

"I don't think it would suit Teddy Taylor to be a tiger," said Granny. "Teddy Taylor's a bear, after all. And the paint mightn't wash off. But I'll be a tiger if you like," she added.

"Yes please," said Ellie.

Granny took her pink hat off again and the painting lady painted a tiger face on Granny. She looked very fierce.

"Are you going to eat me up?" asked Ellie.

"You're a tiger too, Ellie. You might eat me up first," said Granny, putting her pink hat back on.

Just then Ellie saw Mum and Dad. They were not only carrying baby Adam. They were carrying the jar of jam, another jar of honey, the leafy plant, a big book about aeroplanes, an even bigger china dog, a striped green sweater for Dad and two silver balloons for Ellie.

"My, haven't you been busy?" said Granny.

"I never saw a tiger in a big pink sunhat before," said Mum, looking at Granny. "What *have* you two been up to?"

"I took Teddy Taylor on the bouncy castle," said Ellie. "We went on the bouncy castle for hours and hours and hours."

"Adam's too little to go on the bouncy castle," she added. "And Teddy Taylor's too furry to have his face painted." She opened her mouth wide to show her tiger teeth. "But Granny and me are just like *real* tigers!" Ellie said.

*Ellie's feet made a lovely clattering noise when she ran
to the top of the stairs and down again.*

Granny Stays Up Late

Ellie liked going to Granny's house. Though Granny's house was small it was very tall, much taller than Ellie's house. So there were lots of wooden stairs.

There was no carpet on the wooden stairs at Granny's house. Ellie's feet made a lovely clattering noise when she ran to the top of the stairs and down again. Granny didn't seem to mind the noise at all. She let Ellie run up and down as often as she wanted. Sometimes she ran up and down the stairs with Ellie, too.

There were other things Ellie liked about Granny's house. She liked the glass roof, for instance, above the dining-room alongside the kitchen. When Ellie was eating her tea, she could look up and see the sky. She could see the rain bouncing off the roof if it was raining. She could hear it banging on the roof very loudly.

"It looks as if it's going to make us wet. But it doesn't," said Ellie.

The best thing of all, though, in Granny's house was Granny's bathroom. It was much bigger than the bathroom in Ellie's house. And instead of being right against the wall, the bath stood in the middle of the floor and it had feet.

"It looks as if it wants to go for a walk," said Granny.

"Can it come out for a walk with us one day?" asked Ellie.

One day Mum and Dad were going out for

the evening. Baby Adam drank his milk from Mum's breasts, so he had to go too, in his carrycot.

"Good," said Granny. "I'll come round and Ellie and I can have a nice evening all to ourselves."

But then she said, "I've got an even better idea – why doesn't Ellie come and stay at my house, that night?"

"All right," said Mum.

"Can I have tea at your house?" asked Ellie. "And can I have a bath in the walking bath?"

"Of course you can," said Granny.

So next day, before tea, Granny came round to fetch Ellie. She was wearing shiny black trousers and a bright red sweater with little black spots on it.

"You look like a ladybird, Granny," said Ellie.

"It's my ladybird outfit," Granny said.

Ellie had never been away for the night without Mum and Dad. Mum put her nightdress and her dressing-gown and her toothbrush in a little bag.

"Can I take Teddy Taylor and Fenchurch Bear and Maribel Doll and all my other toys?" Ellie asked.

"You can't take them *all*," said Mum. "There isn't room."

"Of course you can. I've got room," said Granny, bringing out a very big bag.

Granny made sardines on toast for tea, Ellie's favourite. She'd bought strawberries and ice-cream. Granny liked sardines and strawberries too. They both had two helpings of everything.

Afterwards they went upstairs and Granny filled up the bath with water, and put bubble bath in until Ellie couldn't see her tummy or her feet.

"Mum doesn't let me have so many bubbles," she said, dabbing bubbles on Granny's nose.

"Well," said Granny, dabbing bubbles on Ellie's nose, "she's a mum. Grannies are different."

"Baths with feet are different too. The bath's not going to go for a walk with me in it, is it?" asked Ellie.

"It only walks when no one's looking," said Granny.

"Good," said Ellie.

When Granny had helped Ellie dry herself, Ellie put on her nightdress and her dressing-gown.

"I've got a pink dressing-gown, too," Granny said. "I like pink."

"Why don't you put *your* dressing-gown

on?" asked Ellie.

"All right," said Granny, putting her dressing-gown on over her red sweater and black trousers.

"Silly," said Ellie. "You don't put your dressing-gown on over your clothes."

"I do. I like being silly," Granny said.

Ellie didn't sleep upstairs next to the bathroom. Granny's bedroom was there. She slept on the next floor down, in the room underneath the bathroom. She arranged her toys round her, took her pink dressing-gown off and climbed into bed. When Granny had read Ellie a story, she kissed her and turned out the light.

"Good night, sleep tight, mind the bugs don't bite," she said. Which is what she always said, saying good night to Ellie.

"Mind the bugs don't bite you, Granny," said Ellie. Which is what she always said back.

"Just call if you want anything else, Ellie," Granny added.

"All right," said Ellie.

She'd felt sleepy up till now. But the moment Granny went out of the room she didn't feel sleepy any more. Even with the sound of Granny's television coming through the wall, the room felt strange to her suddenly. She thought about the clattery stairs, and the dark corner where the stairs turned round. Suppose a ghost lived in the dark? Suppose a ghost started clattering up the stairs? She could almost hear a ghost now.

"Granny," she called, hugging Teddy Taylor. "I'm thirsty. Can I have a drink?"

"Of course," said Granny and brought Ellie a glass of water.

Ellie took a sip of the water and lay down again and tried to go to sleep.

This time she thought of the glass roof in the dining-room. She heard rain falling outside. She remembered the rat-tat-tat-tat sound of the rain on the glass roof. Suppose it broke the glass? Suppose the water filled the dining-room and came all the way up the stairs?

She turned over and over and knocked Mr McTavish off the bed.

"Granny," she called. "Mr McTavish has fallen down."

Granny came in and picked up Mr McTavish again and put him on the bed.

"There's not much room for him with all the other animals," she said. "Perhaps he'd like to keep me company tonight."

"All right," said Ellie.

"Kiss Ellie good night, Mr McTavish," said Granny. And off she went.

Ellie still didn't feel sleepy. And now she

began thinking of the bath with feet in the bathroom upstairs. She didn't like the thought of the bath going for a walk when it was dark. She heard a creak above her head. Suppose the bath was starting to walk *now*? Suppose it wasn't such a friendly bath after all?

"Granny," she called. "Granny. I want you. I want you now."

Granny turned on the light this time. "You should be asleep, Ellie," she said.

"But I don't feel a bit sleepy," said Ellie.

"I tell you what," said Granny. "There's something I make that always puts me to sleep. Put your dressing-gown on, Ellie. I'm going to make some for you."

What Granny made was cocoa. She put a drop of something else in her cocoa, but she said Ellie wouldn't need that to make her sleepy.

"Are there ghosts in your house, Granny?" asked Ellie, sipping her cocoa.

"If there are ghosts, they're nice ones. I'm not afraid of them," said Granny. "But I don't think there are any."

"Nor am I afraid of them," said Ellie. Then she asked, "Suppose the rain falls so hard it breaks the glass roof?"

"This glass won't break," said Granny. "It's special glass."

"Good," said Ellie. Then she asked, "Could the bath really walk, Granny?"

"I don't think so, Ellie. I just like pretending it might," said Granny.

"So do I like pretending," Ellie said.

Ellie didn't feel afraid any more. She liked sipping cocoa with Granny, both of them dressed in pink dressing-gowns.

"Is it the middle of the night, Granny?" she asked her.

Ellie liked sipping cocoa with Granny,
both of them dressed in pink dressing-gowns.

"Well, nearly the middle of the night, Ellie," Granny said.

Ellie did feel sleepy now. And when she went back to bed, she fell asleep straight away.

Next day she said to Mum, "Granny made us cocoa in the very middle of the night. Much too late for Adam to stay up. I expect Adam's afraid of ghosts, too. But we're not afraid of ghosts. Not Granny and me."

"Good," said Mum.

GRANNY IS NAUGHTY

Granny did important work. Sometimes it was so important she had to fly all the way to America in an aeroplane to do it. She sent Ellie postcards from America. Mum had to read them to her because Ellie couldn't read yet. Granny said things like, "Today I climbed to the top of the tallest tower in the world." Or, "Today I met the richest man in the world." Or, "Today I went in the fastest aeroplane in the world."

Ellie liked getting postcards from Granny. But she liked it even better when Granny came home again.

One day Granny came home wearing a

cowboy hat, a fringed leather jacket and a pair of cowboy boots. "Perhaps I'm the oldest cowboy in the world," she said. It was one of Ellie's days to go to playschool. And Mum's day to come with her to help the teachers. But baby Adam had a sniffle. Mum didn't want to take him out.

"I'll go then," said Granny.

"Good," said Ellie. "It's dressing-up day at school today. And you can go as a cowboy, can't you."

"So can you," said Granny, bringing out of her bag a little cowboy hat for Ellie and a red-spotted bandanna to tie around her neck.

"Mind you're not naughty at school today, Ellie," said Mum. "And mind *you're* not naughty either, Granny," she added.

"Of course I won't be naughty," said Granny. She took a tiny leather horse out of her bag and handed it to Ellie. "A cowboy has to have a horse," she said. "I wanted to bring you a real one. But it was too big to go in my bag."

"It would be too big to go in my room, too," said Ellie. "I like little horses better."

"That's all right then," said Granny. She brought out of her bag one more thing – a Pocahontas costume. "You could dress up as Pocahontas," she said.

"I'll take my Pocahontas costume to school for my friend Megan to wear today," said Ellie. "Today, I want to be a cowboy just like you, Granny. Is there time to make a Lego stable for my horse?"

"If you're quick," said Granny.

"You two are going to be late for school if you're not careful," said Mum, as Ellie made her Lego stable. "And last time you took Lego to school you dropped it."

"I'll carry it," said Granny, "I won't drop it." But then she tripped on the front step in her new cowboy boots and the Lego stable fell on the ground and broke.

"I'll help you put it together again, Granny," said Ellie patiently.

"I don't think you two are *ever* going to get to school," sighed Mum.

It didn't take Ellie long to help Granny mend the Lego stable. And then she pretended to ride her horse, all the way to playschool. Granny made cowboy noises.

"Do you think Mrs Prydal will think we're real cowboys?" asked Ellie.

"I'm sure she will," said Granny.

Mrs Prydal was the teacher. "You can try my cowboy hat on if you like," Granny said to her politely. Ellie didn't think, though, that Mrs Prydal looked one bit like a cowboy, even wearing Granny's cowboy hat.

All the other children wanted to try on Granny's hat then, too. And all of them wanted to dress up as cowboys. But Granny's hat was much too big for them. And there weren't any more cowboy costumes. Ellie remembered her Pocahontas costume.

"I don't want to be a cowboy. I want to be Pocahontas," her friend Megan said, as soon as she saw it.

"So do I want to be Pocahontas," said her friend Jed.

"Pocahontas is a girl. You'll have to be Pocahontas's brother," said Ellie kindly.

"Pocahontas didn't have a brother. Not in the film," said Jed.

"Of course she has brothers. And sisters. Lots and lots of them," said Granny. "They just weren't in the film."

So then all the children wanted to be

Pocahontas or Pocahontas's brothers or sisters, except for Louis, who wanted to be Pocahontas's father, Powhatan. None of them wore hats except for Powhatan. Granny showed Louis how to draw and paint feathers for his hat and cut them out, so that was all right.

"Let's play goodies and baddies," said Jed.

"I want to be a goody, not a baddy," said Ellie's friend Megan. The Pocahontas costume looked nice with her red hair.

"Pocahontas is a goody," said Granny. "Only cowboys are baddies."

Ellie pulled her red bandanna tighter, and made her horse gallop at Megan. "I'm a *very* bad cowboy," she said.

"Not *too* bad please, Ellie," said Granny, "or Mrs Prydal won't let me come to playschool again. Remember what Mum said."

"She said *you* weren't to be naughty, either," Ellie reminded her.

"I'll try not to be," Granny said.

When all the children had dressed up, Louis and Seth and Hannah did paintings of Pocahontas. Rosie and Jelila and Tom played in the sand and made a house for Pocahontas and a stable for the cowboys' horses. Megan and Jed and Maia pretended the Wendy House was Pocahontas's House.

"Would Granny like to come in the Wendy House, too?" Megan asked Ellie.

"Granny's too big to go in the Wendy House," said Ellie.

"Oh, no I'm not," said Granny. "Not if I take my hat off."

So Granny crawled into the Wendy House along with Megan and Jed and Maia. She did look funny in a Wendy House with her cowboy boots. There was no room in there for anybody else, though.

"I think I *will* hang my hat up now," she said, crawling out.

But all the pegs outside had the children's clothes on them. So Granny opened a cupboard door looking for more pegs. Only the door wasn't really a cupboard door. It belonged to a little room where Mrs Prydal's dog slept the mornings away while Mrs Prydal was busy being a teacher. Mrs Prydal was always very cross when someone was naughty enough to open the door. Even though usually the dog just wagged his tail and went back to sleep again.

But when Ellie's granny opened the door he didn't go back to sleep. He jumped up and ran out of the little room and into the big playroom, barking excitedly, with Granny chasing after him.

Louis was painting a picture of Chief

*The dog jumped up and ran out of the little room
and into the big playroom, barking excitedly.*

Powhatan. As the dog ran past, his waving tail knocked over Louis's painting water. Trying to catch him, Granny tripped on the sand-tray and smashed down the houses Rosie and Tom and Jelila were making. Then the dog stole one of Megan's shoes that she had taken off when she put on Pocahontas's moccasins. Granny grabbed his collar, missed, and upset Hannah and Seth's jar of painting water. The dog ran round the tables and almost knocked the Wendy House over, too. Until at last he reached Mrs Prydal and jumped up and down in front of her.

Granny, panting, grabbed Megan's shoe out of his mouth at last. "I think he wants to play," she said. "I think he wants to join the playschool."

"He wants to be a baddy, doesn't he, Granny, just like us," said Ellie.

After Mrs Prydal had shut the dog up again, Granny mopped up the painting water, mended the sand houses and straightened the Wendy House. Then Mrs Prydal said Granny could tell the children a story if she liked. So Granny told them the story of Pocahontas. She made it much more exciting than the story in the film. There weren't any cowboys in the film, but there were lots of cowboys in Granny's story – as well as lots of brothers and sisters for Pocahontas. At the end she sang not just one, but two cowboy songs. The second song was "She'll Be Coming Round the Mountain". All the children sang, too. But Granny and Ellie sang the loudest.

Playschool was always nice, thought Ellie. But it was especially nice the day that Granny came.

*   *   *

"I don't suppose Mrs Prydal will let Granny come to school again," said Mum, laughing, when Ellie and Granny told her all about it.

"Mrs Prydal said she can come whenever she wants. Only she must be careful not to let the dog out," said Ellie.

"That's all right then," Mum said.

That evening when Dad came home and asked Ellie what she'd been doing, she said, "I went to playschool and Granny came too. And I wore my cowboy hat and so did Granny wear her cowboy hat. And Granny was so naughty, she let Mrs Prydal's dog out. Mrs Prydal said we were the naughtiest in the whole school, Granny and me."

Granny Plants Cabbages

There was a long thin garden behind Ellie's house. Just outside the back door there was a lawn with Ellie's swing and sandpit, and her paddling pool in summer. She rode her bike up and down the little path alongside. Beyond the lawn there were flowerbeds. And beyond the flowerbeds there was a vegetable garden.

Ellie's dad was proud of his vegetable garden. He grew carrots and peas, lettuces and cabbages, potatoes and beans.

"I don't like carrots," Ellie said. "And I don't like cabbage."

"But you like peas," said Dad.

"And you like potatoes," said Mum. "Especially when I make chips."

Ellie also liked helping Dad in the garden. She helped him hold the hosepipe and water the vegetables. She helped dig the earth with the little spade from her sandpit. Sometimes she helped pull out the weeds. She especially liked pulling out weeds. They came out so easily – except for the dandelions and Dad did those. The only problem was that when the plants were little they looked like weeds too. So Dad didn't let Ellie pull out anything without showing him first.

One day when Dad was digging in the garden Ellie said, "Can I pull out some weeds today, Daddy? *Please*."

But Dad was working much too hard to show her which the weeds were. "Not today, Ellie," he said.

She went indoors to see if Mum would

*One day when Dad was digging in the garden Ellie
said, "Can I pull out some weeds today, Daddy?"*

play with her. But Mum was busy with the baby. "Not now, Ellie. Why don't you look at one of your books? I'll read you the story later," Mum said.

But Ellie wanted a story *now*. She didn't feel like looking at a book all by herself. She didn't feel like building a Lego house either. Or drawing a picture. She took Teddy Taylor and went out into the garden again feeling cross.

Dad had stopped digging. He'd brought a little tray of seedlings out of the greenhouse ready to plant in the bed.

"What are those?" Ellie asked.

"Cabbages!" said Dad.

"Yuk!" said Ellie. "Horrid cabbage."

"But I like cabbage," said Dad. "And so does Mum."

"I don't suppose Granny likes cabbage," said Ellie.

Dad bent down, dug a little hole with his trowel and popped a cabbage plant into it. Then he filled in the hole with earth and patted it down. "That's one cabbage planted," he said, pleased.

He wasn't looking at Ellie. He moved on with his box of seedlings and started to make a second hole.

Ellie bent down and touched the cabbage very gently. "Would it be as easy to pull out as a weed?" she wondered. She pulled very gently. But Dad had patted the earth down so firmly that the plant didn't move. Ellie pulled a little harder. And a little harder. The next instant the plant had not only moved, it had come right out – she had it in her hand.

It *was* fun, she thought. Just like pulling out weeds. She laid the seedling down by the hole and looked at Dad. His back was still turned. He was planting the third seedling.

Ellie looked at the second seedling standing behind him and tiptoed towards it. She put out her hand. In a moment that, too, was lying beside the hole Dad had dug.

Ellie crept towards the third seedling, holding her breath. Dad still hadn't noticed. And she was enjoying herself so much now that she didn't know how to stop. She couldn't resist putting out her hand and pulling this one out as well.

All the way down the row, Ellie remained as quiet as a mouse. Dad kept on digging little holes and planting cabbage seedlings and didn't look round once. While Ellie kept on creeping along behind him and pulling the cabbages out, one by one, as fast as he put them in. It wasn't that she didn't know it was naughty. It was just that she didn't want to stop. Even though she got more and more frightened at the thought of Dad turning round and seeing what she had done.

Dad reached the end of the row. He put the box down and stood up, rubbing his back. Then he turned back to look at his work. Instead of seeing a whole row of little cabbages standing up proudly, ready to grow, he saw a whole row of little cabbages pulled up by Ellie lying beside the holes he'd dug.

"Ellie!" he shouted. "Ellie, you *naughty* girl." He started to run towards her.

Ellie was so frightened now that she ran too, so fast that she was inside the house before he could catch her. She hid behind the sofa in the sitting-room, just in time.

Granny had come to call, though. She was sitting on the sofa. But when Dad came looking for Ellie, she didn't say anything. She just went out into the garden with him to see the naughty thing Ellie had done.

In a little while Granny came back in. She sat down on the sofa again and said, very loudly, "My goodness, Ellie has been busy." She paused. "Poor Dad," she said, "after all that work. Ellie and I had better do some work too. Then perhaps Dad won't be so cross with her, after all. The trouble is, where's Ellie?"

Ellie crept a little nearer the end of the sofa. But she still didn't say anything.

"If I can't find Ellie," said Granny, "Dad will just have to stay cross."

Ellie put her head out from behind the sofa.

"Goodness me," said Granny. "So that's where you'd got to. Come along, Ellie. Let's see what we can do." She was wearing a fluffy brown and yellow sweater today and brown and yellow trousers.

"You look like a bee, Granny," Ellie said.

"Bees like gardens," said Granny.

Ellie and Granny went out into the garden. Down at the bottom, there was the row of cabbages still lying on the ground.

"Let me see," said Granny. "What we want now is a trowel."

Ellie pointed to Dad's trowel lying on the ground at the end of the row. Granny picked it up. "Now, Ellie, how about we plant some cabbages. Though I don't suppose it'll be nearly so much fun as pulling them out."

But it was always fun doing things with Granny. Granny let Ellie help dig the hole. She let her put the cabbage seedling in the hole and then pat the earth down round it. In no time at all they were halfway down the row; in not much longer they had reached the end. And when Ellie looked back all the cabbages were standing up side by side. Only this time she and Granny had planted them.

"I think it's just as nice planting cabbages as it is pulling them out," Ellie said, proudly.

"I think it's just as nice planting cabbages as it is pulling them out," Ellie said, proudly.

"I tell you what's even *more* fun," said Granny. "Planting seeds and watching them come up. On Saturday, Ellie, why don't you come round to my house?"

Dad was still a bit cross with Ellie; but not nearly so cross now his cabbages were planted again.

Next Saturday, Ellie and Mum went round to Granny's house. Granny didn't have a proper garden. But she did have a terrace full of tubs and pots. Granny brought out a little trowel and a paper packet with pictures of flowers on it. Inside the packet were big seeds and little ones, smooth ones, crinkly ones, striped ones, plain ones. Ellie dug tiny holes in the earth in one tub and planted each seed. Then she watered them carefully with a watering-can.

"Will there be flowers tomorrow, Granny?" she asked, looking at the tub very closely to see if the plants were coming up already.

"You have to wait a bit longer than that," said Granny.

"Like I have to wait for Adam to be big enough to play?" Ellie sighed.

"Oh no, Ellie. Flowers grow much faster than babies. You wait and see."

It still seemed a long time to Ellie. But Granny was right. Long before Adam could play with Ellie, her garden was full of flowers – pink, blue, white, even some yellow and orange ones.

"I do like planting flowers," Ellie said. And when Dad brought in one of the cabbages she'd pulled out, and Mum cooked it for dinner, she ate a little bit.

"I thought you didn't like cabbage, Ellie," said Mum.

"I don't like cabbage," said Ellie. "But I like it when I've planted them. And so does Granny. We planted this cabbage, Granny and me."

*When Ellie tickled baby Adam
she could make him laugh.*

GRANNY GOES ON THE SWINGS

Baby Adam was still not big enough to play with. But Ellie could see he was getting bigger, just the same. When she tickled him she could make him laugh. And often when she came into the room, he smiled. "He knows I'm his sister, doesn't he?" said Ellie, pleased.

"Of course he knows you are," said Mum.

"But he still makes dreadful messes in his nappy. Sometimes he does," Ellie added.

"He's getting heavy," Mum said. "Next time we go to the park I think I'll put him in the baby buggy instead of in the sling."

"Teddy Taylor's not too heavy to go in *my* sling," said Ellie.

Ellie liked the park. There was a big sandpit there with a stone crocodile half buried in it. There was a big paddling pool too and three different playgrounds with swings and slides and models to play and climb on, some for big children and some for little ones. Ellie still went on the swings and slides for the little children. But she too was growing bigger.

"I think Ellie's big enough to go on the big swings," said Granny, when she came round one day, and Ellie and Mum and Adam were getting ready to go to the park.

"Are you coming on the swings too, Granny?" asked Ellie.

"I love swings," said Granny.

Today Granny was wearing a pair of blue leggings with yellow spots on and a big yellow sweater. She was carrying something in a big bag.

"What have you got in the bag, Granny?" Ellie asked.

"That would be telling," said Granny, looking mysterious. "Wait and see." And then she added, "But I think it would be a good idea if you brought your bike to the park today, Ellie. For after we've been on the swings."

"All right," said Ellie.

The park was full of people. Mothers with babies in buggies, like Adam. School-children wearing uniforms. Boys playing football. People running in little shorts and big trainers looking hot. People on roller-blades, darting in and out among the walkers and runners, looking much cooler.

"I wish I could rollerblade," said Ellie.

"You can't rollerblade *and* ride your bike," said Granny.

Mum pushed Adam into the baby

playground, because she wanted to sit and talk to the other mothers. Ellie and Granny went off to the bigger children's playground. The sandpit was there and the paddling pool. There was no water in the paddling pool yet, so Ellie couldn't paddle. But she decided to play in the sandpit before they went on the swings.

And so did Granny.

Ellie pretended to ride the stone crocodile, while Granny built a sand wall around it and some fine castles. Afterwards, Ellie's trousers had sand on them. But Granny's blue leggings had a great deal more. Ellie had to brush her down.

"Let's go on the swings now, Ellie," Granny said.

"I want to go on the slide first," said Ellie.

"All right," said Granny. But she looked impatient, Ellie thought.

The slide wasn't big enough for Granny, but Ellie went down it head first. Then feet first. On her back and on her front. Granny thought this was fun, too, even though she couldn't do it.

"Why don't you try going upside down *and* backwards, Ellie?" she asked.

"I think it's time to go on the swings now," said Ellie.

There were two kinds of swings. One had car tyres to sit on. Granny tried sitting on a tyre. She said she didn't think it was quite the right shape for a grown-up, she'd wait to try the other swings. The tyre was just the right shape for Ellie, though. Granny swung her back and forth lots of times, back and forth.

"Harder, Granny, harder," said Ellie.

"But not too hard," she added. Just in case Granny got a little too excited. It was much more fun than the baby swings. She would have liked to go on swinging for ever.

Granny still hadn't had her swing, though. It really was getting to be her turn, thought Ellie, kindly. So she climbed off the tyre and she and Granny went over to the big swings.

They were *much* bigger. Perhaps they are a bit too big, thought Ellie, looking at them anxiously. And they didn't have little seats to fit into like the swings in the baby playground. Suddenly she wasn't quite sure if she wanted to go on these swings after all.

"Shall I lift you on, Ellie?" asked Granny.

"Why don't you have your go first, Granny?" asked Ellie.

"Thank you, Ellie," said Granny.

So Granny had her swing at last. She did look funny, swinging her legs up in their blue and yellow leggings. She wasn't the only granny in the park, Ellie thought, looking around. But she was the only granny wearing blue leggings with yellow spots.

"Isn't it your turn for a swing now, Ellie?" Granny asked.

"You can have another turn if you like," said Ellie.

"Perhaps you'd like to have a go with me, Ellie," said Granny thoughtfully.

"All right," said Ellie. She wondered if Granny meant her to sit on her lap. But Granny was getting up now. And the next thing was she'd climbed on to the seat. And then she was standing on it, holding the chains.

"Come on, Ellie," she said. "Come and sit on the seat and hold on to my legs. And then you'll be quite safe."

So Ellie went and sat on the seat and held tight to Granny's legs. And slowly, slowly, Granny rocked forward and pulled on the

*Granny rocked forward and pulled on the chains
and off they went, higher and higher.*

chains and off they went, higher and higher – but not too high; faster and faster – but not too fast.

"More, Granny, more!" cried Ellie.

"Do you want to wear your granny out?" shouted Granny.

When they'd done enough swinging at last, Granny and Ellie went off to find Mum and the baby. Rollerbladers were still skimming past them on the path. It looked almost as much fun as going on the swings, thought Ellie.

Mum was looking after Ellie's bike for her. She was also looking after Granny's mysterious bag.

"Would you like to see what's in my bag now, Ellie?" Granny asked.

"Yes please," said Ellie.

Granny opened the bag. She dipped in her hand and pulled out a pair of rollerblades.

"Whose are those?" asked Ellie.

"They're mine," said Granny. "I'm just learning. Didn't you notice I was wearing my rollerblading clothes today? Perhaps you'd like to help, Ellie."

"Oh *yes*, Granny," said Ellie, wondering how Granny wanted her to help.

Granny sat down on a bench and put on her rollerblades.

"Get on your bike now please, Ellie," she said at last. Ellie climbed on her bike. And then Granny tied a piece of rope to the back of it and said, "You can pull me along, Ellie, that would be a great help." So Ellie pedalled as hard as she could, while Granny rollerbladed along behind her, holding the rope.

"Don't fall over, Granny!" shouted Ellie.

"I never fall over, Ellie," Granny said.

"I wonder if there are any other

rollerblading grannies," Mum said, when they came back.

"Of course there are," said Granny. "I know lots of rollerblading grannies. I even know a bungee jumping granny."

"I hope you're not going bungee jumping, Granny," said Mum, laughing.

"Not till I'm really good at rollerblading," said Granny.

"I don't suppose other grannies have such lovely rollerblading clothes, or bungee jumping clothes," said Ellie.

"I'm sure they don't," Granny said.

Adam was smiling at Ellie, as usual. Suddenly she had a very good idea.

"If I'm big enough to go on the big swings, do you think Adam's big enough to go on the little ones?" she asked.

"Why not?" said Mum. So she lifted Adam out of the buggy, and Ellie helped strap him into the little swing. And then she pushed him very gently backwards and forwards. Adam laughed and laughed.

"He likes swinging, too," said Ellie. "I knew he would."

Next day at playschool Ellie told all the children, "Yesterday we went rollerblading, Granny and me." Then she added, "Granny and me *and* Adam went on the swings."